PEANUTS®
Make a Trade,
CHARLIE BROWN!

WITHDRAWN

by Charles M. Schulz
adapted by Tina Gallo
illustrated by Robert Pope

Ready-to-Read

Simon Spotlight

New York   London   Toronto   Sydney   New Delhi

SIMON SPOTLIGHT
An imprint of Simon & Schuster Children's Publishing Division
1230 Avenue of the Americas, New York, New York 10020
This Simon Spotlight edition December 2015
© 2015 Peanuts Worldwide LLC
For information about special discounts for bulk purchases, please contact Simon & Schuster Special Sales at
1-866-506-1949 or business@simonandschuster.com.
Manufactured in the United States of America 1115 LAK
2 4 6 8 10 9 7 5 3 1
ISBN 978-1-4814-5688-3 (hc)
ISBN 978-1-4814-5687-6 (pbk)
ISBN 978-1-4814-5689-0 (eBook)

This is Charlie Brown.
He's the manager of a
baseball team.
They have never won a game.
He needs to make a change!

Lucy is the worst player
on the team.
"I'm thinking of making some
changes," Charlie Brown says.
"What kind of changes?" Lucy asks.

"I'm going to trade some players,"
Charlie Brown tells her.
"A few trades can make our team
much better."
"That's a great idea," Lucy says.
"Why don't you trade yourself?"

Charlie Brown calls Peppermint Patty.
"Would you like to trade
any players?" he asks.
"I don't know, Chuck," she says.
"The only good player you have
is the little kid with the big nose."

"You mean Snoopy?" Charlie Brown
says. "Oh no, I was thinking
more of Lucy."
Charlie Brown hears a click.
Peppermint Patty has hung up!

The next day Charlie Brown tells
Linus about the phone call.
"Peppermint Patty only wants
Snoopy. I told her no, but maybe
I was wrong."

Linus is surprised.
"You would trade your own dog just
to win a few ball games?" he said.
Charlie Brown's eyes grew wide.
"Win!" he said. "Have you ever
noticed what a beautiful word
that is? Win! Win! Win!"

The next day Charlie Brown calls
Peppermint Patty.
"I'll trade Snoopy," he says.
"Great!" Peppermint Patty says.
"I'll give you five players
for Snoopy. It's a deal."

Charlie Brown hangs up the phone.
*Good grief! I've traded away
my own dog,* Charlie Brown thinks.
I've become a real manager!

Peppermint Patty has the contract
ready for Charlie Brown to sign.
Charlie Brown is nervous.
"Try not to let your hand shake
so much when you sign the
contract, Chuck!"
Peppermint Patty says.

Charlie Brown has to tell Snoopy. "This is hard for me to say. I've traded you for five new players. Please don't hate me, Snoopy." "Bleah!" Snoopy responds.

Charlie Brown tells Schroeder the news. Schroeder is shocked. "You traded your own dog?" he said.
"Does winning a ball game mean that much to you?"
"I don't know, I've never won a ball game," Charlie Brown replies.

Linus is upset.
"I don't even want to talk
to you, Charlie Brown," he says.
Charlie Brown doesn't say a word.
"And stop breathing on my
blanket!" Linus yells.

Charlie Brown runs back
to Snoopy's doghouse.
"I was wrong," he says to
Snoopy. "I could never trade you!"
"Look! The deal is off." He rips
up the contract in front of Snoopy.

Suddenly, Peppermint Patty
appears at his side.
She sees the ripped-up contract.
"I guess you got my message,
Chuck,"
she says. "The deal is off."

"Those players said they would quit baseball before they played on your team. Sorry, Chuck. I hope you're not too angry," Peppermint Patty said.

"I'm crushed," Charlie Brown says.
But he doesn't really mean it.
He's thrilled! So is Snoopy!
Snoopy is so happy he
starts dancing!

Meanwhile, Peppermint Patty has
a problem with her team too.
Marcie is her right fielder.
She is as bad as Lucy!
"I hate baseball!" Marcie shouts.

Peppermint Patty calls
Charlie Brown with an idea.
"I'll trade you Marcie for Lucy,"
she says.
"Great!" Charlie Brown says.
"I'll trade Lucy for anyone!"

"You traded me for Marcie?" Lucy
says. "You made a terrible
deal. Marcie is awful."
"No, it's a good deal," Charlie Brown
says. "Peppermint Patty threw
in a pizza!"

Marcie loves being on Charlie Brown's team. There is just one problem. She never leaves the pitcher's mound. She likes being close to Charlie Brown!

"Marcie, you're supposed to be in right field," Charlie Brown says. "I'm happier when I'm near you, Charles," Marcie tells him. "I've always been fond of you."

Lucy isn't working out for
Peppermint Patty either.
"Just keep your eye on the ball,"
she tells Lucy.
So Lucy stares at the ball in
Peppermint Patty's hand.

"It's hard to keep my eye on the ball when you keep moving it around," Lucy says.

Later that night Peppermint Patty calls Charlie Brown. "You need to take Lucy back, Chuck!" Peppermint Patty says.

"Why?" asks Charlie Brown.
"Lucy's the worst player I've ever
had," Peppermint Patty tells him.
"But I already ate the pizza!"
Charlie Brown says.

Charlie Brown tells Marcie she's
been traded back to
Peppermint Patty's team.
Marcie is sad the deal is over.

"I guess I wasn't much help,"
Marcie says to Charlie Brown.
"I didn't score a single goal."
Charlie Brown doesn't bother
telling Marcie goals are in
soccer, not baseball!

It's Lucy's first game back
on Charlie Brown's team.
She's holding an umbrella
over her head. A ball bounces
off the umbrella.

"It's not even raining!" shouts
Charlie Brown.
"Not yet," Lucy says.
Suddenly it starts to pour!
The entire team runs for cover,
except for Charlie Brown.

Charlie Brown is getting soaked, but he doesn't care. His team is back together, and they can't lose the game—it's a rainout!